Dear Parent:
Your child's love of reading starts here!

Every child learns to read in a different way and at his or her own speed. Some go back and forth between reading levels and read favorite books again and again. Others read through each level in order. You can help your young reader improve and become more confident by encouraging his or her own interests and abilities. From books your child reads with you to the first books he or she reads alone, there are I Can Read Books for every stage of reading:

SHARED READING
Basic language, word repetition, and whimsical illustrations, ideal for sharing with your emergent reader

BEGINNING READING
Short sentences, familiar words, and simple concepts for children eager to read on their own

READING WITH HELP
Engaging stories, longer sentences, and language play for developing readers

READING ALONE
Complex plots, challenging vocabulary, and high-interest topics for the independent reader

ADVANCED READING
Short paragraphs, chapters, and exciting themes for the perfect bridge to chapter books

I Can Read Books have introduced children to the joy of reading since 1957. Featuring award-winning authors and illustrators and a fabulous cast of beloved characters, I Can Read Books set the standard for beginning readers.

A lifetime of discovery begins with the magical words "I Can Read!"

Visit www.icanread.com for information on enriching your child's reading experience.

*Ree Drummond and Diane deGroat gratefully
acknowledge the editorial and artistic contributions of
Amanda Glickman and Rick Whipple.*

I Can Read Book® is a trademark of HarperCollins Publishers.

Library of Congress Control Number: 2014949456
ISBN 978-0-06-234778-7 (trade bdg.)—ISBN 978-0-06-234777-0 (pbk.)

15 16 17 18 19   SCP   10 9 8 7 6 5 4 3 2 1   ❖   First Edition

CHARLIE
the Ranch Dog
ROCK STAR

based on the CHARLIE THE RANCH DOG books
by REE DRUMMOND, The Pioneer Woman,
and DIANE deGROAT

HARPER

An Imprint of HarperCollinsPublishers

Yawn. Stretch. Ahh . . .

Relaxing with Mama is the best

after a long day of ranch work.

Hey—check out that rock star dog!

Cool shades!

Everyone cheers for him.

His life is so easy!

I want to be like that rock star dog.

No more working my paws to the bone.

Good-bye to Charlie the Ranch Dog.

Hello, Charlie the Rock Star!

The next morning after breakfast,
Mama calls me out to the truck.

Nope. Not today!

Today I'm a new dog.

I need time to hunt

for the perfect outfit.

Look at my mess.

Somebody should clean this up.

Hello? Anyone?

Oh well.

Aha!

Now I'm fabulous.

Here come some of my biggest fans.

My sister and brother will get

all sweaty from ranch work.

But not me!

They say I'm the greatest.

Watch the ears, please!

They have to flop just so.

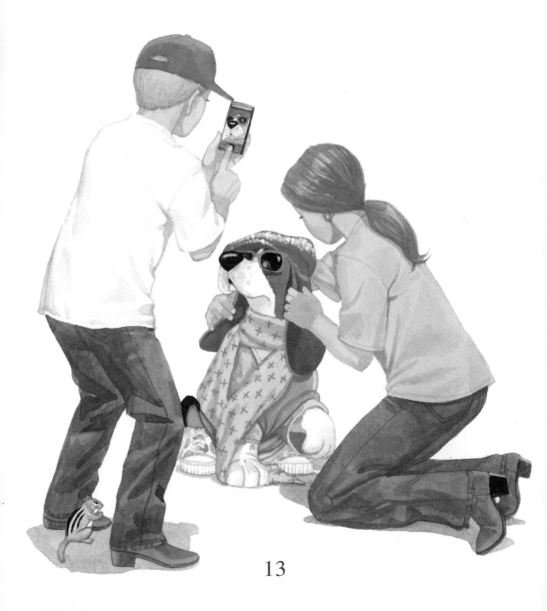

I'm looking sharp.
Now I need a pool,
with a big soft pillow
and a giant umbrella beside it.

I guess my picnic table will do.

Toss. Turn. Ouch!

This table has splinters.

What's that sound?

Oh right!

It's hay-hauling season.

Hay!

Hay isn't as soft as a pillow,

but a dog can dream.

I race out to the pasture.

Daddy is on top of the hay monster.

I hop on for a ride.

I have to try out every bale.

Ouch! This one is too scratchy.

Achoo! This one is too dusty.

Ahhh. This one is just right.

I see Mama in the vegetable garden.

The old me would be by her side,

working away.

But I'm a whole new Charlie.

I'm living the good life.

What's that noise?

Who dares disturb my beauty rest?

A dog can't get a lick of sleep
around this place!

I race around the garden.

Out, you sneaky squirrel!

Get slithering, baby snake!

And you!

This garden is for rock stars only.

I'll chase you out of here, cow!

Uh-oh!

My foot is all tangled up.

Wobble, wobble.

Crash!

Ugh, this scarf!

These shoes!

This stuff really gets in the way.

Hey, where did that cow go?

Finally some sweet silence.

I curl up on a hay bale.

Mama scratches my belly.

She says I chased away every critter

and saved all her vegetables.

Being a rock star isn't that great
after all.

Helping Mama is much more fun.

Mama's got her camera.

One last photo shoot!

Hats are a good look for me.

Get my good side!

Put a piece of bacon in my mouth!

After dinner, it's snuggle time.

My family scratches me all over.

They thank me for my hard work.

The ranch couldn't run without me.

30

The rock star life

isn't as easy as it looks.

Tomorrow I'm back

to being a working dog.

My fans will miss me,

but the ranch life is the one for me.

Time for bacon!